There's a Cow in My House

Words by Brian Steckler

Pictures by Chris Lensch

To my boys, Zane and Nate. - B.S.

To Mom and Dad. - C.L.

First published by Experience Early Learning Company
7243 Scotchwood Lane, Grawn, Michigan 49637 USA

Text Copyright ©2013 by Experience Early Learning Co.
Printed and Bound in the USA

ISBN: 978-1-937954-07-9
visit us at **www.ExperienceEarlyLearning.com**

There's a Cow in My House

Words by Brian Steckler

Pictures by Chris Lensch

experience
Early Learning Company

There's a cow in my house; what should I do?
I tried and I tried to make him go outside.

I pushed and pulled but he sat down to stay.
He said, "Come on, let's play for the rest of
the day!"

**There's a cow in my house; what should I do?
I tried and I tried to make him go outside.**

5

But the cow ate my bread. This is what he said,
"I just need to be fed. Now let's nap on your bed."

There's a cow in my house; what should I do?
I tried and I tried to make him go outside.

When the cow woke up, he took my cup,
and went to the sink to pour himself a drink.

There's a cow in my house; what should I do?
I tried and I tried to make him go outside.

When the sun sank low I said,
"Cow it's time to go."
He said, "I know... and I'll see you tomorrow!"

14

There's a Cow in My House

Words and Music by Brian Steckler

REFRAIN
There's a cow in my house; what should I do?___ I tried and I tried to make him go out-side. _

VERSE 1
I pushed and pulled_____ but he sat down to stay._____ He said,
"Come on, let's play for the rest of the day!"___

REFRAIN
There's a cow in my house; what should I do?___ I tried and I tried to make him go out-side. _

VERSE 2
But the cow ate my bread, this is what he said,_____ "I just
need to be fed, now let's nap on your bed."

experience
Early Learning Company

Experience Early Learning specializes in the development and publishing of research-based curriculum, books, music and authentic assessment tools for early childhood teachers and parents around the world. Our mission is to inspire children to experience learning through creative expression, play and open-ended discovery. We believe educational materials that invite children to participate with their whole self (mind, body and spirit) support on-going development and encourage children to become the authors of their own unique learning stories.

www.ExperienceEarlyLearning.com